STUART·LITTLE™

Search and Find

📕 **HarperFestival**®
A Division of HarperCollinsPublishers

Search and Find
© 1999 by Columbia Pictures Industries, Inc. All Rights Reserved.
Adapted by Justine and Ron Fontes
Illustrated by Rivoli Design Group
Colorized by Brian Harrold
HarperCollins®, ☰®, and HarperFestival® are registered trademarks of HarperCollins Publishers Inc.
All Rights Reserved.
ISBN 0-694-01417-6
Library of Congress catalog card number: 99-62455
http://www.stuartlittle.com
http://www.harperchildrens.com

**Stuart Little is very small,
so take a careful look
and see if you can find him
on every page of this book!**

Stuart is going to the Littles' house.
Can you search and find
this tiny mouse?

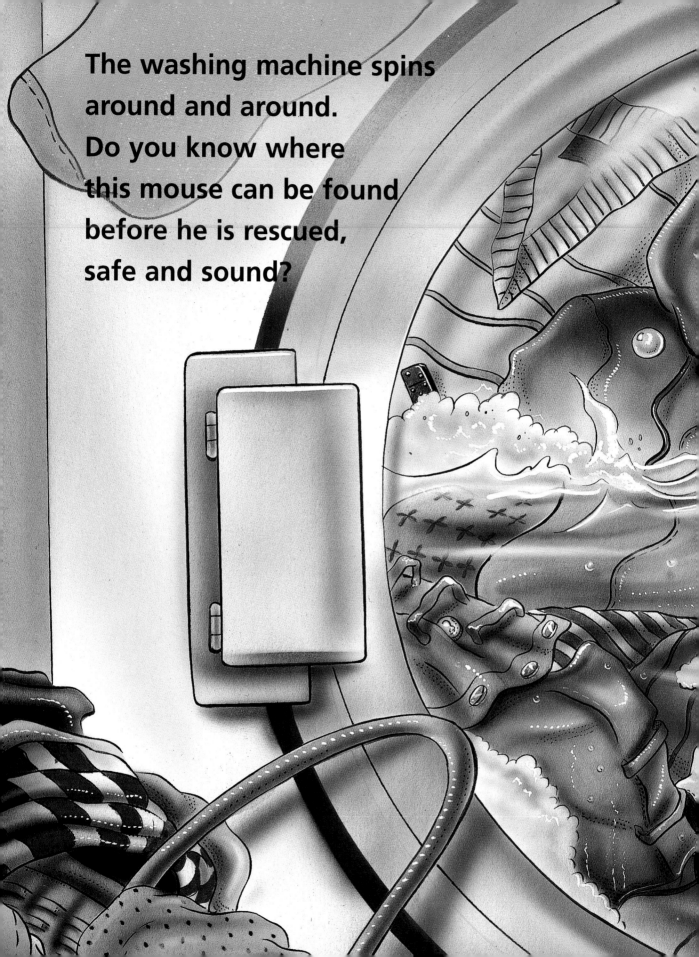

The washing machine spins
around and around.
Do you know where
this mouse can be found
before he is rescued,
safe and sound?

The Littles welcome him
with presents and cheer.
Do you know if little Stuart is here?

Snowbell doesn't like
his new little master.
Do you know where Stuart is?
Will there be a disaster?

Stuart's brother has
a model train, boat, and car.
Can you tell if Stuart Little
is near or far?

The boat race begins.
The competition is tight.
Is Stuart among them?
Is he left . . . or right?

Now Stuart must leave
and live with the Stouts.
Can you find him here?
Is he wandering about?

In the end, Stuart returns
to his true family.
Can you search one more time
for where Stuart might be?

Now turn back the pages
and start once again.
Search for these items
until it's the end!

a hot dog

a pretzel

a soap bubble

a key

a spinning top

a pair of dice

an hourglass timer

a bird

a cowboy

a spool of thread

an anchor

a clothespin

a yo-yo

a baseball cap

a glove

a whistle

a thimble

a seashell

a sheriff's badge

an airplane

a square of cheese

a wheelbarrow

a set of binoculars

a kite

a pair of serpents

a fish

a star

a shoe

a harmonica

a quarter

a mouse's name

a marble

a spoon

a message in a bottle

a clock

a domino

a butterfly

a sunset

a playing card

a candle

a jack

answer key

STUART

an airplane

a hot dog

a butterfly

a pretzel

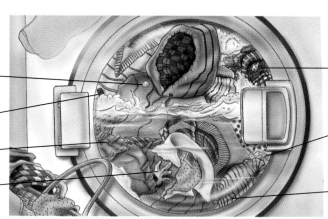

a soap bubble

a domino

a quarter

a glove

STUART

a key

a marble

a spinning top

a pair of dice

a cowboy

STUART

a harmonica

a mouse's name

STUART

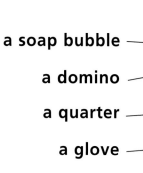

a clothespin

an hourglass timer

a spoon

a thimble

a square of cheese

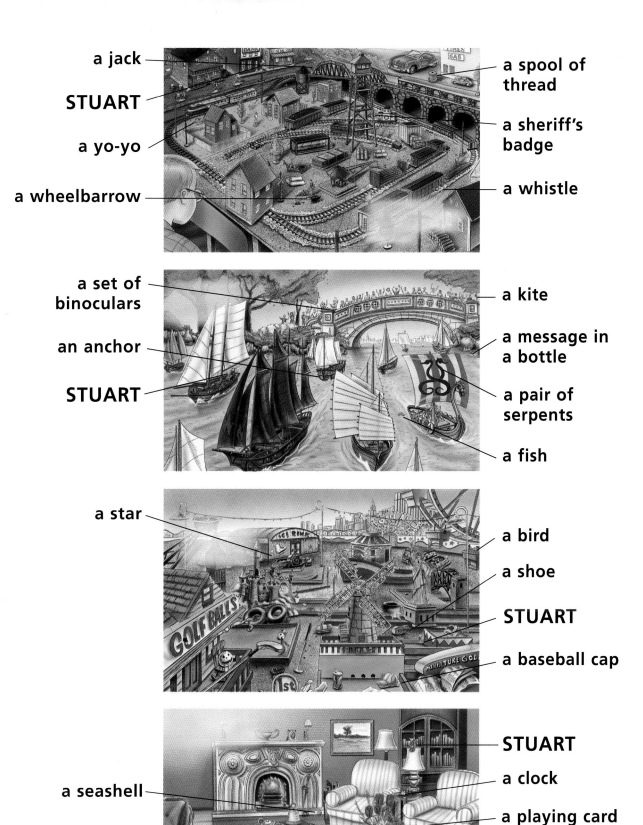